E
GIL

CUENTO
DE LUZ

To my mother, a glowing great-grandma, who overflows with the joy of living.
- Carmen Gil -

To all of those who bring light into our lives.
- Silvia Álvarez -

STONE PAPER®

Water and tear resistant
Produced without water, without trees and without bleach
Saves 50% of energy compared to normal paper

Daisy
Text © 2017 Carmen Gil
Illustrations © 2017 Silvia Álvarez
This edition © 2017 Cuento de Luz SL
Calle Claveles, 10 | Urb. Monteclaro | Pozuelo de Alarcón | 28223 | Madrid | Spain
www.cuentodeluz.com
Title in Spanish: Margarito
English translation by Jon Brokenbrow
Printed in PRC by Shanghai Chenxi Printing Co., Ltd. February 2017, print number 1604-2
ISBN: 978-84-16733-32-3

Daisy

Carmen Gil
Silvia Álvarez

This is a story about a donkey. Well, a donkey, a mule, or a burro. What a lot of names! And she answers to them all. But the name she likes the best is Daisy.

One spring morning, many years ago, a little donkey raised her soft muzzle into the air for the first time, and saw a beautiful meadow full of flowers.

"We'll call her Daisy," said her owner. The little donkey brayed—or laughed. It's difficult to tell with donkeys.

From that day
on, Daisy became a part
of the family. She helped to bring in
firewood, she played with the children, and she took
them for walks. And all day and all night, she kept a close watch
to make sure the wolf kept away from the farm. Thanks to her
long ears, she was always the first one to hear him.
When she did, she would bray loudly,
until her owners came
running.

Daisy was happy with her life. She loved her work, and she was so proud to be a donkey! A donkey, just like the one in the story "The Musicians of Bremen." A donkey, just like the one who had accompanied Sancho Panza on his adventures with Don Quixote. A donkey, just like the one who had helped to keep the baby Jesus warm in the stable in Bethlehem.

On the farm, Daisy was everyone's friend. The sheep would bleat happily when they saw her, because she protected them from the wolf. The cows mooed when Daisy fanned them with her ears. The chickens clucked away merrily between her legs when they shared her feed. The dog would bark when he played with her tail. Even the cat purred loudly when she lay on the soft hair on Daisy's back.

And so, to the sound of bleating, mooing, clucking, barking and meowing, the years went happily by. Daisy was fifteen years old. Then she was twenty. And then she was thirty. As she got older, she gradually became weaker, deafer, and less agile. She couldn't jump over the fence without stumbling, she couldn't carry much firewood on her back, and she couldn't hear the stealthy footsteps of the wolf as he crept around the farm.

One rainy afternoon, a beautiful pony arrived at the farm. He was young and full of life, and all the animals looked at him with amazement. His name was Dazzle, and he was very proud to be a horse. Just like Pegasus, who had flown through the skies on his mighty wings. Just like Silver, the faithful companion of the Lone Ranger. Just like Bucephalus, who had conquered half the world with Alexander the Great.

And the sheep bleated happily, because now they had a new protector. The cows mooed as they admired his youth and energy. The chickens clucked at his feet, pecking at the oats he dropped. The dog barked when Dazzle tossed him a ball of hay with his muzzle. Even the cat meowed, as he rode on his back.

Dazzle was thrilled. He loved being admired. He would leap over high walls to show how agile he was. He would carry heavy bundles of firewood to show how strong he was. And he would whinny when a visitor was still miles away, amazing one and all with his superb hearing. Meanwhile, Daisy looked on from a corner of the farmyard, forgotten by everyone.

Summer arrived, and the owners of the farm set off on vacation. While they were away, Dazzle would show off to all of the animals, galloping and leaping into the air. He was so full of energy that he accidently tipped over the drinking trough. All of the water poured out, and was quickly absorbed by the soil.

"What are we going to do now? We're all going to die of thirst!" said the terrified animals.

The sheep bleated for help in their pen. The cows mooed for help in the meadow. The chickens clucked in their henhouse. The dog barked next to the gate. The cat meowed from the rooftop. Even Dazzle whinnied in fear from inside the stable. Meanwhile, Daisy looked on from her corner of the farmyard.

"If each of us calls for help on their own, nobody will hear us. We have to work as a team," said Daisy.

"As a team? What's that?" clucked the speckled hen.

"It means all together," explained Daisy. "We'll all call at the same time, so that someone can come and help us."

Well, with all the mooing, whinnying, barking, meowing, clucking, and bleating, it didn't take long for the neighbors to hear them and come running.

"Don't worry," said Mr. Thomas, puffing through his long white beard. "We'll have that drinking trough fixed in a jiffy, and we'll fill it up with water."

And soon, everything was back to normal.

The animals drank and drank until the water was sloshing around in their tummies, and thanked the donkey for her advice.

"Thanks to your wisdom, you've saved us all!" they said. Daisy brayed happily—or chuckled. You never know with donkeys.

From that day on, everybody in the farm turned to Daisy when they needed help and advice. There wasn't a problem, however complicated, that the clever little donkey couldn't solve.

Oh, and all of the animals decided to form a choir. They traveled around delighting everyone with their songs. Of course, Daisy was the conductor, and she kept them all in time using a baton made out of an olive branch.

So you'd think that Daisy was just as happy as a donkey could possibly be. Well, believe it or not, something happened that made her life even more joyous than ever before.

A family moved into the neighboring farm, with a little boy with long, straight hair, a short neck, slanting eyes, and a nose that looked just like a saddle. His name was Danny. When they met, Daisy and Danny became the very best of friends. If you happen to pass by, you can see them walking together. If you get even closer, you'll hear the old donkey telling Danny funny stories about when she was young, and you'll see Danny smiling and chuckling. And you'll hear Daisy braying away—or laughing. You can never tell with donkeys.